TV
Stars!

The
Sleepover
Club

Have you been invited to all these sleepovers?

The Sleepover Club Best Friends
The Sleepover Club TV Stars
The Sleepover Club Dance-off!
The Sleepover Club Hit the Beach!

Coming soon...

The Sleepover Club Pet Detectives
The Sleepover Club Hey Baby!

TV

The SleePover Club

Stars!

Fiona Cummings

HarperCollins *Children's Books*

First published in Great Britain as *Sleepover Girls on Screen*
by HarperCollins *Children's Books* in 1999
This edition published by HarperCollins *Children's Books* in 2008
HarperCollins *Children's Books* is a division of HarperCollins*Publishers* Ltd,
77-85 Fulham Palace Road, Hammersmith, London W6 8JB

www.harpercollinschildrensbooks.co.uk

1

Text copyright © Fiona Cummings 1999

Original series characters, plotlines and settings © Rose Impey 1997

The author asserts the moral right to be
identified as the author of this work.

ISBN-13 978-0-00-726493-3
ISBN-10 0-00-726493-3

Printed and bound in England by
Clays Ltd, St Ives plc

Mixed Sources
Product group from well-managed
forests and other controlled sources
www.fsc.org Cert no. SW-COC-1806
© 1996 Forest Stewardship Council

FSC

FSC is a non-profit international organisation established to promote the
responsible management of the world's forests. Products carrying the FSC
label are independently certified to assure consumers that they come
from forests that are managed to meet the social, economic and
ecological needs of present and future generations.

Find out more about HarperCollins and the environment at
www.harpercollins.co.uk/green

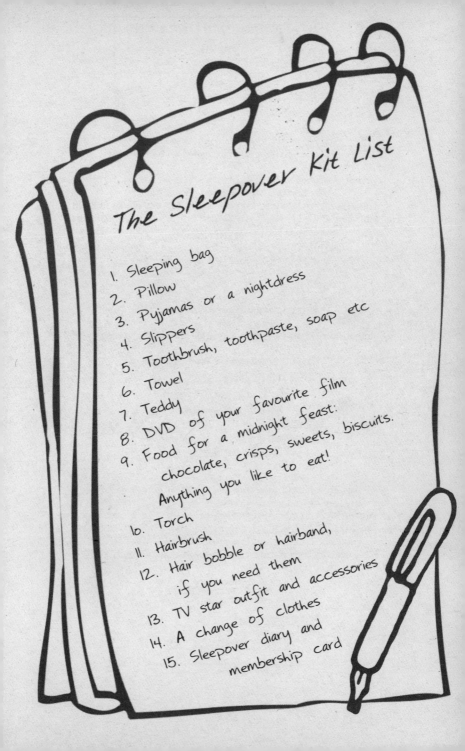

The Sleepover Kit List

1. Sleeping bag
2. Pillow
3. Pyjamas or a nightdress
4. Slippers
5. Toothbrush, toothpaste, soap etc
6. Towel
7. Teddy
8. DVD of your favourite film
9. Food for a midnight feast:
   chocolate, crisps, sweets, biscuits.
   Anything you like to eat!
10. Torch
11. Hairbrush
12. Hair bobble or hairband,
    if you need them
13. TV star outfit and accessories
14. A change of clothes
15. Sleepover diary and
    membership card

1

Did someone just call my name? I could have sworn that I heard someone shout "Lyndz"!

Oh hi! I didn't see you there. I'm glad you're here. Do you think you could give me a hand with this scenery? The Sleepover Club are putting on a play in my garden. It's just for our parents but it should be pretty cool. We wrote it ourselves, so we could play exactly the parts we wanted.

Fliss is going to be a princess who ends up marrying a handsome prince – surprise, surprise!

7

You know how she loves a good wedding! And of course dressing up is like her favourite thing in the whole world. Come to think of it, most of Fliss's clothes are all frilly like a princess's. And she acts like royalty too – most of the time she thinks that our Sleepover Club stuff is way too childish for her.

Kenny is going to play a footballing genius who scores the winning goal in the FA Cup. Don't ask how that fits in with the princess, it just does. She said that she wouldn't be in the play at all unless she could be a footballer. Kenny's greatest love in life is Leicester City and she really thinks she's going to play for them one day – as well as being a doctor like her dad. When she's not being a footballer in the play, she's lots of different monsters and villains as well, but we tell her that she can't really call that acting! You know Kenny – she's a bit wild at the best of times, so a lot of people think she's a monster anyway. But it's her *sister* who's the real monster – Molly the Monster, as we call her.

Rosie plays sort of a Cinderella character who triumphs against the odds, and that's kind of like Rosie too. When she came to Cuddington at first she was all sort of lost and didn't really fit in. Her dad had just left and she was finding it quite hard to cope. Now she's one of our best friends and is really sensible and gets things organised.

She doesn't get things as organised as Frankie though – now *she* can be really bossy. That's why she fancies herself as the director of our play. She's also its narrator, which is a really important role. She fills in as different characters too and sort of holds the whole thing together. I sometimes think it's Frankie who holds the Sleepover Club together, because the rest of us would fall out too much if she wasn't there.

What character am I playing? Well, I dash around on a horse a lot helping people out. I said I didn't mind what role I played as long as it was something to do with horses. I live for horses! We haven't got a *real* horse in the play of course. Sometimes Kenny pretends to be my horse and I ride on her back, but we usually end up collapsing in a heap on the floor.

Frankie said that I should be a kind of magical character who always does good things, because she says that I'm always nice to people in real life. I don't know about that. She hasn't seen some of the awful things I've done to my four horrible brothers!

You're looking a bit confused. I know all this play stuff sounds a bit strange, but you see, we've caught the acting bug. *Big* time! It's all Fliss's fault really. I know, I know – poor Fliss seems to get the blame for everything. But this time, I mean it in a good way.

You know how she's always going on about wanting to be a supermodel? For all those nice clothes, that fame and stuff? Well then, it shouldn't surprise you that one day she announced that she wanted to become an *actress* instead. Actress, supermodel – it was all the same to Fliss.

10

"I'll still be famous and earn loads of money," she explained, "but there's not the same pressure on you to be beautiful all the time, is there?"

The rest of us rolled our eyes. I mean, what is she *like*?

"I don't think you can just decide to be a famous actress and *wham* – you've got the starring role in the next *High School Musical*," said Frankie. "You've got to go to drama school first."

"And I've heard that most actresses are usually out of work," continued Rosie. "There's only a few who make it to the top."

"Well, I'm going to be one of those!" said Fliss firmly. And when Fliss is in one of those moods, there's no arguing with her.

So for the next week or so we had to put up with her prancing about with her actress head on. Whenever Mrs Weaver asked her something in class, Fliss would take a deep breath, smile and speak v-e-r-y s-l-o-w-l-y and very clearly. The first time she did it, Mrs Weaver said:

"Are you feeling quite all right, Felicity?"

The rest of us nearly wet ourselves laughing. But Fliss didn't care. She just seemed to be acting all the time, as though her life was being filmed for one long soap opera.

Kenny thought it would be a laugh if we all started acting too – or maybe that should be *over*acting… So Frankie would say something like, "I say old beans, can I interest anyone in a game of rounders?" and Rosie would reply, "Oh super! A game of rounders would be simply spiffing on such a wonderful warm afternoon!" And we would all clap our hands and do really false laughs. It was like some really bad over-the-top crackly old movie. It was great fun though. Fliss got really cross with us at first.

"Acting's not like that!" she snapped. "You're supposed to be natural!"

"Oh like you, you mean!" snorted Kenny. She put on a really posh voice and started to speak really slowly. "Of course I know what five times six is, Mrs Weaver. It's forty-six of course!"

The rest of us cracked up.

"I never said that!" said Fliss crossly. "I know that five times six is thirty!"

We laughed even harder.

"Oh Fliss, where's your sense of humour?" giggled Frankie. "We're just saying that you seem to be taking this actress thing a bit far. If you're so keen, why don't you go to a drama class? There's got to be one somewhere near here."

That sounded like a great idea. At least that way we wouldn't have to suffer Fliss trying to be the next Lindsay Lohan. Or so we thought...

It was just our luck that when we went to Brownies a couple of days later, someone had put up a brand new poster on the notice board. It was luminous yellow so it sort of hit you right in the eyes. It said:

Starstruck?

Dreaming of a career
on the stage?

Or just want to have some fun?

Then this is the class for you!

Drama classes with Angel

Wednesday evenings
6 – 7pm
St. Mark's Church Hall,
Cuddington
STARTS 26th MAY!

£2
Per class

"Look at that!" said Fliss, hopping around from foot to foot as she read it. "Don't you see? It's a sign! I wanted to go to a drama class and suddenly there's one right here on our doorstep! We've *got* to go to it! It's going to make me a star!"

"Hang on a minute!" insisted Kenny. "What's all this *we* business? It's *you* who wants to be the actress. You're on your own!"

Fliss pouted and made her eyes all big and wide. She's always doing stuff like that to make people feel sorry for her, but it doesn't usually work with us.

"Actually, it might be a laugh," admitted Frankie. "My gran's always calling me a 'little actress'. It might be kind of fun to go to a proper drama class."

"Well I've always fancied being a TV presenter, and I guess a few drama lessons might help," said Rosie. "Then I might get a big break myself and end up presenting *Blue Peter*. That would be so cool!"

15

"The point is that going to drama class would be good for all of us," said Fliss seriously. "Come on, let's all go, it'll be great! Please? Pretty, pretty per-lease?"

Before we had time to decide, Brown Owl came in and we had to get into our packs. The poster definitely gave us a lot to think about, though. Fliss, Frankie and Rosie all seemed really keen on the idea of going to drama classes, and I was certain that Kenny would go too – she'll do anything for a laugh. I wasn't sure that it was exactly my kind of thing, but was I going to miss out? No way!

After the Brownie meeting Fliss was still excited about the drama class.

"You will all be able to go, won't you?" she kept asking.

"Oh Fliss, give it a rest!" groaned Frankie. "We'll ask when we get home. OK?"

I knew that Mum and Dad wouldn't mind me going, as long as it didn't affect my school work. As it was kind of near the end of term anyway, I couldn't see that happening. Unfortunately my stupid brothers found out about the drama class too, and wouldn't stop taking the mickey out of me.

"You might get a part in one of those vet programmes," suggested Stuart my eldest brother, who helps out on the local farm whenever he can.

"Yeah, as one of the animals!" laughed Tom. He's fourteen, so you'd think he might be a bit more mature than that. Listening to Ben and Spike laugh, you'd think he'd cracked the funniest joke ever. But I suppose when you're four like Ben, anything's funny – and Spike is only a baby, so he doesn't know any better.

Still, their endless teasing about me trying to act really got on my nerves, and I thought about not going to the drama class after all. Of course I didn't, because when I saw the others the next day they were still all really up for it and we always tend to do stuff together.

So the next week, on Wednesday 26th May,

we found ourselves at St. Mark's Church Hall in Cuddington, not really knowing what to expect. But you know what? It was the start of one of our craziest adventures yet!

To be honest with you, I didn't really know what to expect from the drama class. I kind of hoped it would be like *Fame Academy* with loads of cool kids strutting about, but that kind of thing is never really going to happen in Cuddington!

"So what do you think we'll be doing in this class?" asked Rosie, looking about her nervously. We were waiting outside the hall with a few other people. The doors were locked, which wasn't a good sign.

"Never mind what we're going to be doing, are you sure there *is* a class here?" said Kenny, looking a bit fidgety. "I'm going to give this another five minutes, then I'm off!"

"It's only six o'clock now," said Fliss. "There's no need to be so impatient."

"I hate waiting around," Kenny replied through gritted teeth, and went to climb the tree behind the hall.

"Well that's not going to impress the drama teacher very much, is it?" sniffed Fliss. "I don't know why Kenny always has to be such a fidget."

It's true that Kenny is kind of impatient and wants everything done yesterday, but I guess we were all getting a bit twitchy. It's the 'fear of the unknown', as Dad sometimes says.

I looked around at the other people waiting. Most of them were about our age and most of them were girls. I recognised quite a few of them from Brownies. There was a small group of older children who all seemed to know each other too. One of them looked very like one of Tom's mates,

Daniel. I kind of wanted to go up to him to say "Hi", but I felt too nervous and wimped out.

Suddenly there was this enormous bang and a sort of spluttering sound. A really battered old car had come to a halt just outside the hall.

"Hey, look at that!" whispered Rosie.

"It looks as though it's going to fall to pieces at any minute!" breathed Frankie.

We were all busy staring at the car when this bright red shape stepped out of it and stood in the road, beaming at us. It was a woman with loads of purply-coloured hair piled on top of her head.

"That, my darlings, is known as making an entrance!" she laughed. She had this incredibly deep voice and the most fabulous earrings, which looked just like birds hovering above her shoulders. The group of older children burst out laughing and clapped really loudly. Fliss looked both embarrassed and annoyed with them at the same time.

"Ah thank you, my loyal fans!" The woman

shrieked with laughter. "You know how I love an audience! Now Daniel, can you help me with my things? You too, Sophie. And the rest of us had better get inside."

She marched up to the door and tried to push it open. It wouldn't budge because it was locked. *We* all knew that, but she just didn't seem to believe it. As she heaved her body against it, everybody had a good look at her. She was wearing all these floaty layers of clothes. Her skirt came to her ankles, and so did the long waistcoat she was wearing over the top of it. They were both bright red, but her top underneath was orange. I'd never seen anyone wear colours like that together before. When she turned round to smile at us we could see that her lipstick was a deep red, and she had painted black lines above her eyelashes. She looked kind of exotic.

"Do I have the key?" she asked, as if that was something we should know. I guess we all looked a bit blank, because she started to rummage in her enormous handbag.

"I suppose I must have, let me see now!"

All sorts of things started spilling on to the ground: a fat notebook with all its pages hanging out, a Mickey Mouse purse, three lipsticks (one without a top), a chequebook covered in gooey red stuff (lipstick probably) and finally a fat bunch of keys.

"Ah, here we are!" she said triumphantly, holding them up for us all to see. "Now which do you suppose opens the door?"

"We'll be here all night!" muttered Kenny, who had reappeared at the sound of all the commotion.

Frankie and Rosie looked as though they could hardly believe their eyes. But they weren't giggling or anything, which is what we normally do. They looked totally engrossed. Fliss was looking a bit apprehensive, but then when you have a mum who's as organised and colour-coordinated as Fliss's, I expect seeing someone so outrageous is a bit of a shock to the system.

By this time Daniel had stepped forward, found the right key and opened the door.

"In we go, in we go, in we go!" sang the woman.

When we were all finally in the hall she introduced herself.

"My name's Angel, and it's fab to see so many of you here. Some of you I know…" (she turned to smile at Daniel and his friends) "but lots of you I don't. So let's all introduce ourselves to each other."

First of all we had to go round and say hello to everyone and tell them what we were called and how old we were. Then we had to sit in a circle and take it in turns to introduce ourselves to the whole group. Rosie got a bit panicked about that and her words wouldn't come out at all. She sounded as though she'd swallowed a dishcloth. Angel was really brilliant though, she didn't get angry or anything. She was really reassuring and told her that it was OK to be nervous. Besides, a few of the other kids clammed up too.

Kenny wasn't nervous at all. When she introduced herself, she said that the most important thing in the world to her was football. You could tell by the way she said it that she thought drama classes were just a bit of a laugh.

"You know, that's really interesting, Kenny," said Angel when she'd finished, "because I always think that acting's a lot like playing football."

Kenny's ears pricked up as soon as she said that!

"Footballers train all week for one match, don't they? Well, actors rehearse for a play and then they're on, in front of a crowd. It's the same adrenalin buzz. Actors have to react quickly to situations, just as footballers have to know which shot to make when two defenders are haring towards them."

Kenny was *definitely* interested now. As long as something's similar to football, it's all right with her!

After that, Angel split us up into smaller groups. We all made sure that we were together, and Juliet, one of the older girls, came to join us.

"How do you know Angel?" Frankie asked her.

"She did a drama workshop at school," Juliet told us, "and it was so great that I started doing the courses she runs at weekends and in the holidays."

"Do you go to Cuddington Comprehensive?" asked Rosie.

"Sure do!"

"Do you know Tom Collins then?" I asked.

"Oh don't tell me that you like him too! Isn't he gorgeous? I think he'd make a really good actor. He looks a bit like Brad Pitt, don't you think? I keep trying to persuade him to come along to the workshops, but he won't!" declared Juliet with a giggle.

Kenny and Frankie were both sniggering. I couldn't believe that my stupid brother could have such an effect on girls. I mean, Juliet *looked* normal enough, but there must be something seriously wrong with her if she fancied Tom.

But before I could say anything, Fliss shrieked, "Lyndz doesn't *like* Tom – he's her brother!"

You ought to have seen poor Juliet's face. Talk about beetroot! She just didn't know where to put herself. For the rest of the class she was sort of distracted and didn't take much part in the role-playing we were doing.

When we left she came up to me and said, "Don't tell Tom what I told you, will you? But try to persuade him to come along to the class next week."

Yeah, right! Some hope! The last place he would want to be is somewhere with his kid sister. And I wouldn't want him to come anyway. I was definitely going to go back though, because we'd had a totally cool time. Angel was great and everybody was really friendly. The others thought so too.

"That was so *fab*!" squealed Rosie, who had got over her dishcloth mouth.

"What did I tell you!" said Fliss smugly. "I *knew* it would be brilliant!"

"And Angel seems to know a lot about football too," said Kenny admiringly. She started to speak like Angel, in a really deep voice. "If we go on like this we'll be starring in the next blockbuster movie – no problem, darlings!"

For the next week we pretended to be Angel all the time. We even tried to perfect her laugh, which was sort of all thick like treacle.

The drama classes were our highlight of the week. We were doing something we were all interested in, and we were doing it all together. For once we were all happy and we didn't fall out at all.

Well, surprise, surprise – that didn't last for long!

For the first couple of weeks, everything we did at Angel's drama class was completely new to us. I'd thought we might have to learn loads of lines for a play, and I'm no good at that. In school plays I always end up as a tree or something because I'm hopeless at remembering lots of words. Well, Angel's class wasn't like that at all. We did loads of improvisation exercises which were really great. Sometimes we split into twos, and one of us was a hairdresser and the other was the client who'd just been given a disastrous perm. Or we were in a big group and we had to act out an emotion, like being happy or sad, and everyone had to guess what it was and then copy what we'd done.

One class was *so* funny. Angel asked us to pretend that we were angry ducks. I know that it sounds weird, but Angel likes to make you look at the world a bit differently. Anyway, everyone in the class was waddling around the room quacking in people's faces. It was a riot. Well, when I say everyone, what I mean is everyone except Kenny. *She* was making screeching noises and going "BEEP BEEP!" at the top of her voice. It was hil-*arious*.

Eventually Angel stopped the class and asked Kenny to show everyone her interpretation.

29

Well there she was, screeching and beeping, and everyone just fell about laughing.

"That's very interesting Kenny," said Angel, trying not to laugh herself. "Can you just remind everybody what that was?"

Kenny looked kind of embarrassed. "An angry truck," she said. "Isn't that what you wanted?"

Frankie and I just totally collapsed into fits of giggles. It's a wonder I didn't get hiccups.

"That's what I thought she'd said," explained Kenny, sounding a bit injured when she came to sit down next to us.

"Didn't you realise that everyone else was pretending to be a *duck*?" gasped Rosie, still holding her sides and giggling.

"I was so into being a truck, I didn't notice what anyone else was doing," admitted Kenny. "But I was good, wasn't I?"

We had to agree that she was the best angry truck that we'd ever seen!

It was after about the third drama class when Angel called us all together.

"I've got some very exciting news!" she said in her deep throaty voice. She was wearing a big beaded choker and it moved up and down on her neck as she spoke. "How would you fancy auditioning for a television advert?"

There was a stunned silence. Then the hall kind of exploded.

"Really?"

"Excellent!"

"Fantastic!"

"What's the advert for?" asked Frankie, who always gets down to the serious stuff first.

"Good question!" said Angel, smiling at her. "I'll be able to give you more details next week. All you need to know at the moment is that the advertising company are looking for a 'bright, sparky girl who is approximately ten years old'."

That description covered most of the drama class. I looked around and everybody was chattering eagerly with their friends about it. Juliet smiled at me and came over.

"You lucky thing, I wish I was ten again. Fancy being able to go up for a commercial when you've only been coming to drama classes for a few weeks," she said. "You sound like just the kind of person they're looking for too!"

She was just being kind to me because I was the wonderful Tom's sister, but it was nice of her to say that anyway. When she'd gone back to her friends I joined the others.

"Just imagine," Fliss was saying, "I'm going to my first audition!" She patted down her hair as though a casting director was watching her already.

"Well if it's bright and sparky they want, they won't have to look any further than me!" Kenny pranced up and down the hall.

"Not if they see me first!" Frankie bumped her out of the way.

Angel was getting ready to lock up so we all bundled out of the door.

"'Bye darlings, see you next week!" she called after us.

By the time we got outside, Fliss was totally hyper about the whole thing.

"Don't you see? It's another sign!" she shrieked. "First I tell you that I want to be an actress and Angel's drama class pops up, and now she tells us about this audition. It's like this part already has my name on it! What do you think?"

"I think you'll have some competition from the rest of us," said Kenny. She sounded quite serious too. I didn't say anything.

Dad picked us up in the van and dropped everybody off. And all the time Fliss was twittering about the stupid audition for the advert. The more she went on about it, the more sure I was that *I* didn't want to go for it. And what a big mistake *that* proved to be!

3

I guess I should explain why I didn't want to audition for the commercial. I'll try, but to be honest I'm not a hundred per cent sure myself. It was more a sort of feeling I had, really. I know that I usually just go with the flow, but this time I didn't want to. I suppose the problem was that I couldn't face my brothers teasing me about the audition. You know what they're like. They just go *on* and *on* about things and never let them drop. That's OK sometimes, like when they tease me about spending so much time with horses. But with other things – like this TV commercial – well, it's just not worth the hassle.

I didn't mention anything about the audition to Mum or Dad because they'd have made me go for it. Even though I didn't want to. They like me to stand up to my brothers you see. But it was one thing keeping my decision from my parents. It was quite another keeping it from my friends.

I was really panicking when I went to school the next morning. I knew that the commercial was all they would be talking about and I didn't want to feel left out, but I didn't want to lie to them either.

Sure enough, when I got into the playground Fliss was already in full flow.

"I'm going to smile at the advertising people like this…" (she did this big cheesy grin) "because Mum says that then they'll be able to see that I'm bright and sparky, and that I have good teeth."

"I bet they will!" muttered Frankie.

"They'll probably barf up their breakfast, more like!" grinned Kenny.

Fliss ignored them. "This means a lot to me," she said firmly. "You know how much I want to be an actress."

We all rolled our eyes.

"I'm not sure how I'm going to approach it yet," chimed in Kenny. "Should I do this?" She pulled down the corners of her eyes and stuck out her tongue. "Or what about this?" She curled back her top lip until it was touching the base of her nose.

"You're *so* gross!" laughed Rosie. "I think being natural is probably best."

"I'm sure Angel will tell us what the advertisers are looking for," said Frankie. "We'll probably practise in class anyway."

I hoped that we wouldn't... but at least I didn't have to say anything to the others because the bell went for the start of school.

When we were in school we couldn't talk

about the audition, but as soon as break time came the others started up again.

"Can you imagine being on television every night?" asked Rosie. "Everybody would see you!"

"Yeah, even some big film producer! He might give you a part in his next movie." Kenny whirled about as though she was in some big fight scene.

"Hey, maybe we'll get our own show!" shrieked Frankie. "*The Sleepover Show!*"

We all cracked up laughing.

"You're not really going to audition, are you?" asked Fliss.

"Sure am!" replied Kenny. "It sounds like a right laugh. Why, don't you think I'm good enough?"

"It's not that," said Fliss slowly, "it's just that you're, well – a bit of a tomboy, aren't you? They usually have girly girls in adverts. You wouldn't want that, would you?"

Kenny looked a bit put out at this. Fliss smirked ever so slightly, and turned to Frankie.

"What about you Frankie, are you going for it?"

37

"Yeah, it'll be great experience," admitted Frankie. "Even if none of us gets the part."

"Hmm," said Fliss, looking Frankie over. "Don't you think you're probably a bit tall? You look so grown up, they're never going to believe that you're only ten."

Frankie thought about that.

"Well I only look ten," Rosie piped up, "and I'll do anything once."

"You get a bit nervous though, don't you?" said Fliss kindly. "I bet an audition will be really scary."

She turned to me. "What about you Lyndz?" she asked.

"Nah, I'm not going to audition," I spluttered. "It's not really me, is it?"

"Of course it's you!" yelled Rosie.

"If we're doing it, you've got to do it!" said Kenny.

"She doesn't have to if she doesn't want to," said Fliss quickly. "Lyndz knows that she doesn't really want to be an actress, and she'll just be wasting the advertising people's time if she goes along to the audition."

Everyone went a bit quiet.

"Ohhh… I get it," snarled Kenny all of a sudden. "You're trying to put us all off because you want the part yourself!"

"But I *am* the one who wants to be an actress," whined Fliss. "You only came along to the class because I asked you to."

"Yes, and now we've decided that we want to audition too," said Kenny firmly. "There's no rule saying that we can't be actors too, you know."

The others were silent. We all looked from Kenny to Fliss, expecting major fireworks, but they just glared at each other. I was relieved when the bell went for the end of break, but I knew that we hadn't heard the last of their little feud.

The awful thing was that in a way, I was glad that Fliss and Kenny had fallen out, because it kind of took the pressure off me. Everybody was so worried about them arguing that nobody seemed too bothered that I wasn't actually going for the audition myself.

The bad feeling between Kenny and Fliss also meant that everybody was really careful not to mention the audition at all. I had thought that they would be going on about it the whole time – but whenever someone even mentioned television, Frankie, Rosie or I quickly changed the subject. So by the time the drama class came round again, Kenny and Fliss were just about speaking to each other and almost seemed to have forgotten why they had fallen out in the first place.

On the Wednesday evening, I met Frankie outside the hall.

"I'm not looking forward to this," she admitted.

"Why not?"

"Because World War Three's going to break out again between Fliss and Kenny as soon as Angel mentions the audition," Frankie reminded me.

Rosie came to join us.

"Maybe we shouldn't audition either," she suggested. "You've probably got the right idea, Lyndz. It might cause too much aggro if we're all competing against each other."

"But that's like backing down!" said Frankie indignantly. "If we want to audition for the commercial, then we should. If one of us gets the part, the rest of us should be happy for her. We're too old to be spoilt babies!"

"Maybe you should tell that to Fliss and Kenny!" suggested Rosie.

"Tell what to Fliss and me?" asked Kenny. We hadn't seen her before because she'd been creeping along the side of the wall, you know, like they do in American detective programmes.

"Erm, tell you that…" spluttered Rosie, looking anxiously at Frankie and me.

"We should tell you that it's about time we arranged another sleepover," I said on a brainwave.

Kenny looked at me as though I was mad. "Yeah, right," she said, looking dead suspicious.

"Hey, here's Fliss now," yelled Rosie, relieved at the distraction.

Sure enough, there was Fliss, done up like a dog's dinner in her best jeans and enough eyeshadow to decorate the inside of the hall. One look at her was enough to remind Kenny about their stupid feud.

"They're not casting for the advert today, you know!" she hissed. "So coming all done up like that won't help you!"

"There's no harm in looking smart," Fliss snapped back.

Frankie, Rosie and I all looked at each other and pulled faces.

"Come on, we'd better get inside," said Frankie quietly, and in we went.

We always started the class with a few warm-up exercises, then we went into improvisation work. Angel put us into pairs, and always put us with a different person every week. That particular week she paired me with Frankie, which was great. But who else do you think she paired together? Yep – Fliss and Kenny!

"Oh no," moaned Frankie when she saw what

Angel had done. "Of all the weeks for her to have put those two together!"

Fliss and Kenny were glaring at each other like two panthers waiting to pounce.

Angel started to explain the exercise to us. "OK, one of you has taken your friend's homework without asking. When you give back the book, it's all filthy and covered in stains. It looks like you've dropped it in the mud and some of the pages are ripped. The friend can't hand it in like that, and will have to spend the whole night copying it out again. Decide who is to play each role – and *go*!"

I love doing improvisations like that! Frankie and I really got our teeth into it. I imagined how I'd feel if that happened to me. We were reasoning with each other when we heard this really heated conversation behind us. Fliss and Kenny were both bright red in the face and yelling at each other at the top of their lungs.

"They're going to kill each other in a minute," Frankie whispered.

Angel clapped her hands.

"Now that's what I call real aggression!" she said. "Fliss and Kenny, let's listen to your argument."

I held my breath. I was kind of hoping that they'd be too embarrassed to carry on in front of the rest of the class – but no such luck!

"You always think you're so special, don't you?" yelled Kenny. "You think everybody else should just back down and let you do whatever you want!"

"No I don't. I expect a bit of cooperation from my friends though!" screamed Fliss.

"You're just frightened of finding out that you're not Miss Perfect after all!"

"That's just rubbish!"

"OK, right, OK." Angel clapped her hands hurriedly. "I think you've strayed from the basic argument there, girls, but that was very good! Right, we'll swop partners and try that exercise again!"

And she swiftly moved Fliss and Kenny as far apart as she could.

Towards the end of the class, Angel called for all the ten-year-old girls to join her in a group.

"She's going to tell us about the advert," squealed Rosie excitedly.

Angel took a piece of paper from her bag.

"OK, this is the moment that you've all been waiting for."

An excited murmuring spread through the group.

"Auditions will take place on Saturday 25th June at the rehearsal rooms in Leicester from 9.30am. It's an open audition so I advise you to get there early."

"But where are the rehearsal rooms?" someone asked.

"And what will we have to do?" Fliss called out.

"What's the advert for?" Kenny shouted louder.

Angel looked amazed. "Gosh, I'm not doing this very well am I?" she laughed. "I'd forgotten that I hadn't given you any details about the commercial. Here goes." She read from the sheet of paper. "The advertisers of *Spot Away*, a new cleanser for teenagers, are looking for a ten-year-old girl to appear in their new commercial. She must be of average height and build, have a bright, bubbly and expressive face and dark hair."

A wave of noise sort of built up amongst us. There were a few nervous giggles.

"Spot cream?" squealed Kenny.

I started to laugh. I mean, *really* laugh. Tears were streaming down my face and I was doubled up. Then of course I got the dreaded hiccups. It was just so funny, them getting all excited about an advert for *spot cream*. The others all started laughing too. But then an awful sort of shrieking cut through the giggles. It was Fliss. She was clutching her hair.

"But I've got blonde hair!" she wailed. "What about me?"

4

Even Kenny was upset to see Fliss so distressed. We rushed over to where she had crumpled into a heap on the floor. But at least my hiccups had stopped. It must have been the shock of Fliss's wailing.

"I want you to take some deep breaths, Fliss, like we do at the start of the class," Angel told her very calmly. "In, out, in, out – that's it. Can you feel your breathing getting calmer now? Good."

The whole class by this time had crowded

round. Everybody was looking anxiously at Fliss.

"Right, I want everybody to sit down," said Angel softly, her deep voice still filling the room. "And that includes you older guys."

Everybody just sat where they were. Rosie handed a tissue to Fliss, whose eyes were all red.

"Now this is a very good time to give you all some good advice," said Angel slowly. "Acting is a very fickle profession. Sometimes it doesn't matter how good an actor you are – if your look isn't right, you don't get the job. It's as simple as that. I know that's not fair, but it's a fact of life. That's why acting is so tough and very few people make it to the top."

She looked round at us all. "This class is supposed to be fun, you guys. I don't want you stressing over it. Fliss has just had a tough break because her look doesn't fit." Fliss's eyes started to well with tears again. "But next week something might come up where the casting director is looking for petite blonde girls and she'll fit the bill perfectly."

Fliss smiled weakly.

Angel continued, "We can't all be winners all the time – and that's a good lesson for everyone to learn. That's life!"

There was a ripple of subdued laughter.

"For those of you who are keen on going for the audition, we'll do some preparation work for it next week. The address of the rehearsal rooms is on these leaflets." She passed them round. "There's also my home phone number at the bottom. If anyone's parents want to give me a ring to ask me any questions, please tell them to feel free. And on that note, guys, I bid you adieu!"

Everyone started chattering and headed for the door. A couple of the older girls were talking to Fliss, telling her how something similar had happened to them.

"Poor Fliss," I said. "She really wanted to go for that audition."

"I know!" Frankie agreed. "I feel a bit guilty that we can all go for it and she can't."

"Maybe we shouldn't," said Rosie quietly.

Kenny said nothing. She just looked over to where Fliss was lapping up all the attention she was getting.

When Fliss finally came to join us, she was looking a bit more cheerful.

"Everybody's been really kind," she sniffed. "They knew how upset I was."

"I bet the whole of Cuddington could hear how upset you were!" muttered Kenny. Frankie dug her hard in the ribs.

Dad was waiting for us outside in the van. I climbed in first and whispered to him, "Don't ask us about the class whatever you do!" I think we'd all had enough weeping from Fliss for one day.

We didn't say much as Dad drove round dropping everyone off. It was a relief when everyone had got out and there was just me and Dad left.

"Do you want to talk about it?" he asked.

I shook my head. If I told him about Fliss, I'd have to tell him about the audition. Then I'd have to explain why I didn't want to go for it myself. It was best to keep quiet.

We had two more days at school before the weekend. That meant two more days of avoiding the subject of the commercial.

"We can't go on like this forever," whispered Rosie, as we were tidying the classroom on Friday afternoon. "It's silly not even *talking* about the audition. Fliss is going to have to face up to it sometime. I mean, what's she going to do at drama class next week when everyone's practising for it?"

"Worse than that." Frankie bent down next to us to pick up some bits of paper from the floor. "Kenny is still determined to audition for it herself."

"Oh no!" We all looked over to where Kenny was furiously sweeping the floor. She was trying to sweep up the M&Ms (Emily 'the Goblin' Berryman and Emma 'the Queen' Hughes) with all the rubbish, which was kind of funny.

"What are we going to do?" I asked.

Frankie shrugged her shoulders.

"There's nothing we can do. At least Fliss will have the weekend to get over it. Hopefully she'll be OK about everything next week."

I hoped so. I really, *really* hoped so.

Before I tell you whether she was or not, do you think you could help me lift this bit of scenery over here to the bottom of the garden? It's going to go in front of the climbing frame to make it look like a castle. What do you think? It's good isn't it? Rosie designed it.

Now what was I saying? Oh yes, I was telling you about Fliss wasn't I? You're going to love this!

Usually we all meet up sometime over the weekend, but that particular weekend we didn't. I don't really know why not. We must all have been doing different things with our families, I guess. Anyway, on Monday morning I was kind of looking forward to meeting the others at school. To be honest with you, I'd tried not to think about the whole audition thing. I just hoped that Fliss was OK now, and that if Kenny and the others did decide to go for it, Fliss wouldn't cause too much of a fuss. But knowing Fliss, that was probably too much to hope for.

I was a bit late getting to school on Monday – as usual – and by the time I got into the playground the bell was already ringing. I could see Frankie, Kenny and Rosie walking in just ahead of me, but there was no sign of Fliss.

"Hiya!" I ran up to them. "Where's Fliss?"

"Dunno!" shrugged Kenny. "She's probably taken to her bed because life is so unfair!" She pretended to swoon on to the benches in the cloakroom.

"You idiot!" laughed Frankie. "It is a bit odd that she's not here though. She must be ill."

In the classroom Mrs Weaver was standing by her desk talking to a girl. We couldn't really see who it was because she had her back to us, but she wasn't anyone we recognised. She was kind of small and thin and had long dark hair.

53

"Who's that?" I mouthed to Frankie. She pulled an 'I don't know' face.

I was expecting Mrs Weaver to tell us all that we had a new girl in our class. But instead, the girl, keeping her head down, walked over to sit next to Rosie. We all looked at each other. That was *Fliss's* seat.

"Erm, I think you've made a… FLISS!" yelled Kenny.

Fliss was no longer blonde. Now she had chestnut-coloured hair and she looked, well – different.

"What have you done?" squealed Rosie.

"Dyed it," muttered Fliss.

"So you can do the audition for the TV commercial?" I asked.

Fliss nodded. Kenny was tapping the side of her head to show that she thought that Fliss was crazy. Frankie gave her a warning look, so she stopped.

"Did your mum do it for you?" asked Rosie. She couldn't stop staring at Fliss's hair.

Fliss nodded. "Mum tried to get through to Angel to talk to her about the audition but her phone was always engaged. So she dyed my hair for me at the weekend. I'll be used to it by the audition on Saturday, and the advertisers will think it's natural."

It was obvious that the rest of us thought she was crazy, but of course we didn't say anything. And when the stupid M&Ms started teasing her about it, we all stuck up for her. Pop stars change their image all the time, don't they? So why not Fliss?

At drama class on Wednesday night we were all just about used to it, but poor Angel didn't know what to make of it at all. She kept telling Fliss that doing something so drastic wasn't really the best idea and that it certainly wouldn't guarantee her success. Of course Fliss wouldn't listen to that. Once she's set her mind on something, nothing will shift her.

Angel made us all practise for the audition. I suppose she did that so that nobody felt left out. It was quite simple really. All you had to do was hold a bottle of *Spot Away*, pretend that you were with your older sister and say: "So this is why you spend so long in the bathroom!"

Angel said that in the advert there would then be a voice-over about how *Spot Away* works. Then the camera would come back on to the two sisters, the older one would say something rude, and the younger one would pull a face and stick out her tongue. We were all very good at that bit!

After we'd done that a few times, we broke up and did other improvisation exercises, but you could tell that everyone's mind was really on the audition. If I'm honest, I couldn't see what everybody was getting so excited about. It was hardly some award-winning piece of television. It was an advert for spot cream, for goodness sake!

Before we left, Angel advised all those girls who were going to the audition to practise handling products as though they were advertising them on the television. Apparently it's one of the things casting directors look for. She said that she would see people at the auditions and wished everybody luck.

When we got outside Fliss was all excited.

"I've been dying to tell you guys all evening that Mum says she'll take us all to the audition on Saturday!"

"Cool!"

"And she said that we might as well have a sleepover at my place the night before!" she squealed. "Then we can practise everything and we'll all be nervous together!"

"Who's going to be nervous?" asked Kenny.

"ME!" screamed Rosie and Fliss together.

"You will audition now, won't you Lyndz?" Frankie turned to me.

I shook my head. "Nope."

"Well there's no point you coming to the sleepover then, is there?" said Fliss.

I don't think she'd meant it to come out like that, but the others all looked really shocked.

"That's a bit rude, Fliss!" Frankie turned on her.

"We always have our sleepovers together. We can't have one without all of us there," reasoned Rosie.

"You'll just have to audition after all, Lyndz!" laughed Kenny.

"No thank you," I said. To be honest with you, it sounded as though it would be an awful sleepover. The others would be practising their stupid stuff all night. Then Fliss would start panicking and Kenny would make fun of her. Nope, I'd be better off away from that. Still, I felt a bit upset because we *did* always have our sleepovers together and I didn't really want to miss out.

"I only thought that Lyndz might get bored," said Fliss quickly. "Of course I want her to come."

"And you won't have to audition if you don't want to," said Rosie kindly.

"I know!" yelled Frankie all of a sudden, "you can come along to the audition with us and be our lucky mascot!"

"Yes!" the others cheered.

They all grabbed hold of me and we danced around in a big huddle. So that was settled then. I must admit that I felt pretty chuffed at the idea of being the Sleepover Club mascot. But all the same, I had a bad feeling about the whole thing. I couldn't help thinking that something was going to go terribly wrong...

5

Things went a bit wrong for me before I even got to the sleepover. I was in kind of a mad rush to get all my stuff ready on Friday night. It's better really if we have our sleepovers on Saturday because then you can take your time preparing for them. On Fridays, we get in from school and then have to get ready to go out again and there's usually not enough time. Anyway, on that Friday I was just glugging down a glass of juice in the kitchen when Tom appeared.

"Who's going to be advertising zitty skin cream then?" He threw his sports bag at my feet.

"What are you talking about now?" I asked, trying to sound cool. How on earth had he found out about the commercial? Then I remembered – Juliet!

"A little bird told me that you're going to an audition tomorrow," Tom continued.

"Well your little bird told you wrong. I'm not going for it actually," I hissed. Mum was outside and I didn't want her to hear.

"Embarrassed about advertising zit cream are you?" he sniggered.

"No," I replied. "But if I had spotty skin like yours, I might be."

Tom blushed. I felt a bit mean. He hasn't really got many spots, but he's dead embarrassed about the little ones on his chin.

"I'm going to tell Mum anyway," he said nastily.

I felt bad because I'd told Mum that Mrs Sidebotham, Fliss's mum, was taking us into

61

Leicester for the day, but I hadn't told her why. My heart started thumping.

"I am not going to the audition," I said. "But if you open your big mouth at all, I'll tell everybody about your 'little bird' Juliet, and how much she fancies you."

That shut him up. But I had a panicky feeling in my stomach all the time I was getting my stuff together.

The thing with parents is that they're always one step ahead of you. As Dad drove me to Fliss's later, he asked, "Why didn't you tell us about the audition?"

I couldn't *believe* that Tom had grassed on me before I was even out of the house.

"I'm going to kill Tom," I muttered.

"It's nothing to do with Tom. Fliss's mum rang this afternoon and told us where she'd be taking you tomorrow," Dad explained. "She asked us why you didn't want to audition too. I had to tell her that we didn't know anything about it, but I said we were sure that you had your own reasons."

I didn't know what to say.

"I guess I just didn't want to make a fool of myself," I eventually tried to explain. "Do you mind?"

"Not at all, love. You have to make your own decisions about these things," Dad smiled. "You should know that we'd never make you do anything you don't want to."

"Does that mean that I won't have to do my maths homework again?" I asked.

"Don't push your luck!" Dad laughed.

We pulled up outside Fliss's.

"Have a good time," Dad said. "And remember, you're always a star to us!"

I gave him a kiss and jumped out of the van. I felt sort of relieved that Mum and Dad knew about the audition. I don't like keeping secrets from them.

Fliss's mum appeared at the door before I'd even had a chance to ring the bell.

"Late again, Lyndz!" she said with a bright smile. "Take your shoes off, there's a love. The others are upstairs in Felicity's room – rehearsing."

We've always got to take our shoes off when we go into Fliss's house, but it always feels weird. That's probably because I'm not used to it. In our house if you don't wear your shoes, you'll probably step in something nasty. But Fliss's home is always ultra clean. The carpets are all cream and soft and fluffy. It's kind of like walking on a cloud.

I left my shoes by the others in the hall, grabbed my sleepover stuff and followed the noise upstairs.

"So that's why you always spend so long in the bathroom," Fliss was saying, slowly and clearly. I opened her bedroom door and was greeted by the others all sticking their tongues out at me.

"Hiya Lyndz!" Frankie rushed over and grabbed my stuff from me. "You're going to be sleeping on the floor next to me and Kenny."

"This is *my* sleepover if you don't mind." Fliss pushed her out of the way. "*I* should show my guests where they'll be sleeping."

"Ooh la-di-da!" Kenny squawked, and stuck her tongue out at Fliss's back. I don't think she was rehearsing for the audition either!

Fliss's room is very like Fliss – all pink and neat. She has two beds, both with exactly the same covers. Rosie's stuff was already on the spare one and Frankie had put my sleeping bag beside hers on the floor. I put my bag next to it and Fliss straightened them up. Then she asked anxiously, "Should we practise our lines again?"

"Give it a rest Fliss," moaned Kenny. "We've already been through them about ten times."

"Well, will you help me decide what to wear tomorrow then?" asked Fliss, throwing open the doors of her huge wardrobe.

We all groaned. Fliss makes us look at all her clothes every time we have a sleepover at her place. This time, she couldn't decide between a pale pink mini and white skinny-rib top or a short fitted navy dress.

"Well what do you think?" she asked, for about the hundredth time in Sleepover Club memory.

"I think you're really sad," said Kenny seriously.

The rest of us started to giggle. Fliss looked upset.

"Come on Fliss, she's only joking," soothed Frankie. "But can't we go out in the garden or something? It's such a lovely evening, and we've been up here for ages."

Boy, did it feel good to be out in the fresh air. We acted like a bunch of three year olds who hadn't seen daylight before. We whooped and cheered and ran about like maniacs. We made so much noise that Mr Watson-Wade, Fliss's gruesome next door neighbour (or Mr Grumpy, as we call him), popped his head over the fence.

"Do you think you girls could keep it down a bit?" he moaned. "We're trying to get baby Bruno off to sleep and it's simply impossible with all this noise!"

We said that we were very sorry. Then, when we knew he'd gone inside again, we screamed with laughter and made more noise than ever. It was *ace*. We love annoying Mr Grumpy!

Before he could complain again, Fliss's mum called out, "Supper time!"

I like my food, as you know, but at Fliss's you never really know what to expect. Her mum tends to do lots of fancy stuff – dainty little sandwiches cut into stars, tiny little tartlets and weeny bits of pizza. She probably thinks that if she cuts all our food up small, there's less chance of us making a mess.

After supper we went back upstairs and – guess what? The others started rehearsing for the audition again. Fliss has a television in her room and whenever any adverts came on Fliss would scream and point and we all had to watch them to see if we could pick up any tips! It was *dead* boring, and I wished that I hadn't come to the stupid sleepover after all.

But things started looking up when Fliss said that maybe they ought to practise with some real spot cream. Her mum is a beautician so she always has loads of lotions and potions lying about. Fliss went into the spare room where her

 67

mum sees all her clients, and came back with a basket piled high with all sorts of jars and bottles. She put it on her bed and we all dived in.

"Hey, look at this anti-wrinkle cream!" yelled Kenny, opening a jar and slopping some on her face.

"What about this?" shrieked Frankie. "It says it's for 'firming and refining'. I'll have some of that!" She whacked a great dollop of it on her arms and some of it spilt on to Fliss's bed.

"Watch it!" snapped Fliss anxiously. "I don't think we should be doing this!"

"It was your idea," said Rosie, who was smearing some violet-coloured cream over her cheeks. "Ooh, try this, you guys – it makes your skin go all tingly!"

"All I meant was that we should practise *holding* some jars, in case we have to do it at the auditions tomorrow. Mum's going to kill me if she finds out that we've been using her stuff."

"Don't worry, she won't," I tried to reassure her. "We'll put everything back and she'll never know."

68

"Let's just keep one bottle to practise with," suggested Frankie. "What about this one? It looks kind of like a spot cream." She took a small bottle from the basket.

"OK," agreed Fliss. "Help me put the rest back, will you?"

We piled all the jars back into the basket and Fliss hurried back into the spare room with it. She was just coming back when Callum, her stupid seven-year-old brother, bounded up the stairs. He'd just come home from his mate's house.

"What were you doing in Mum's room?" he asked immediately. "You know that you're not supposed to go in there."

"Shut up, weasel!" Fliss hissed. "If you tell Mum, you're dead, do you understand?"

Fliss is like a different person when she's with her brother. You know, sort of normal. Callum pulled a face and went into his room.

"What if he tells on me?" she wailed.

"He won't," said Kenny, "… if he knows what's good for him."

Fliss looked reassured, and snatched the bottle from Frankie.

"Let me practise with that then," she said, "and you can be the older sister."

They pretended that the mirror on Fliss's dressing table was the camera and they acted into that. Kenny shouted "Action!" and they pretended they were filming. Frankie and Fliss practised a few times, then Kenny and Rosie had a go. Then they started making up their own adverts, which was even funnier. They used the skin cream and pretended they were advertising that, smoothing it all over their faces and saying how brilliant it was. Even I joined in with that.

Fliss was just giving it all she'd got when her mum came in. Fliss jumped about a mile.

"Bedtime, girls!" said Fliss's mum brightly. Then she frowned, sniffing the air. "There's a very strange smell in here... Oh no!"

She had seen the bottle in Fliss's hand.

"Not my orchid and rose-oil cream!" she shrieked. "Have you any idea how much this costs?" She snatched the bottle from Fliss's hand. "*How* many times do I have to tell you not to go into my room, Felicity? I am disappointed in you. If you still want to go to the audition tomorrow, I suggest that you all get ready for bed now. I don't want to hear another sound out of you, is that clear?"

We all nodded. Fliss's mum stormed out of the room and Fliss burst into tears.

"Don't worry Fliss," Frankie reassured her. "If we go to bed now, she'll have forgotten all about it in the morning."

We grabbed our stuff and crept along to the bathroom. Fliss has this amazing whirlpool bath which we usually mess about in, but that night we didn't dare. We had a wash and brushed our teeth as quickly as we could. Then we crept back to Fliss's room.

"We'd better have our midnight feast now, before Mum comes upstairs," Fliss suggested, in a subdued sort of voice. It was kind of early, but we're always ready to eat, so we grabbed our goodie bags and poured them out on Fliss's bed.

"Mmm, I love dolly mixtures," mumbled Kenny, munching into about twenty. "Wouldn't it be cool if we could advertise *them*!"

"Yeah, or chocolate!" laughed Frankie. "I reckon I'd keep getting it wrong, just so I could keep eating more of it!"

"No, the best would be advertising Pepsi with Boyzone, what do you think?" suggested Rosie, pretending to swoon on her sleeping bag.

There was a knock at the door. Andy, Fliss's mum's boyfriend, popped his head round.

"I think I should warn you that your mum's still on the warpath Fliss," he grinned. "If I were you I'd think about turning out the lights and going to sleep. Night all!" He closed the door again.

Fliss started to look a bit wibbly again, so I said, "That's OK Fliss, I'm getting kind of tired anyway. Besides, you lot need your beauty sleep – you've got a big day ahead of you tomorrow. You don't want huge bags under your eyes do you?"

"And you'd better not cry any more," Kenny

said to Fliss. "Your cheeks are all red and blotchy."

Fliss put her hand to them. "That always happens when I cry," she said. "Do I look really awful?"

"No worse than usual!" the rest of us said together.

We all crawled into our sleeping bags and Fliss turned off the light. I think the others turned on their torches and started to sing our Sleepover song, but I can't really remember because I must have fallen asleep. Audition day was nearly here – and no-one that night could have predicted how it would turn out!

The next morning I woke up really early. I *always* wake up early – it drives the others mad. I usually have to start singing or something to wake them up too, but this time I didn't have to. It seemed like I was just about the last to wake up, apart from Kenny of course. She'd sleep all day if she could.

"I hardly slept last night," muttered Rosie from the depths of her sleeping bag. "I couldn't help thinking about the audition. I'm sure I'm going to mess it all up."

74

"No you're not!" said Frankie firmly. "Like my gran always says, we can only do our best."

"Did you sleep, Fliss?" I asked. She was all sort of tangled up in her duvet, but we knew she was awake because she kept twitching about.

"Not really." She turned towards us and sat up. "If I'd known the rest of you were awake we could have practised for the audition again."

The rest of us didn't reply. We were all too busy staring at her...

"What's the matter?" she asked irritably. "Why are you looking at me like that?"

Frankie recovered first. "We just can't believe you wanted to rehearse some more in the middle of the night!" she said quickly.

Fliss just sighed. "I'm going to the bathroom," she said, and got up.

As soon as she was out of the room, Frankie, Rosie and I turned to each other.

"Did you see her *face*?" squealed Rosie. "Her skin's all blotchy! She'll *die* when she sees it."

"She's going to be so upset," I said, really

75

worried. "What if she won't go to the audition? What will you lot do then?"

Just then Kenny sat up. "What's all the noise about?" she mumbled. "Why are you awake so early? It's not time to get up, is it?"

Before we could answer, there was a loud scream from the bathroom. We all looked at each other.

"Fliss has just looked in the mirror," Rosie said.

"What's up with her?" asked Kenny curiously.

Then Fliss ran back into the bedroom, waving her arms around and howling.

"*You're* covered in zits!" exclaimed Kenny in amazement. "You're going to be a right one to advertise *Spot Away*, aren't you?"

Good old Kenny really knows how to put her foot in it. Fliss collapsed sobbing on to her bed. We all leapt out of our sleeping bags and went to comfort her.

"They're not spots, they're only blotches Fliss," Frankie tried to reassure her. "Maybe it's nerves or something."

Kenny then came over all doctor-like and tried to examine Fliss's face.

"It looks like a rash," she said.

"Oh well done, Kenny, we'd never have guessed," snorted Rosie sarcastically.

Kenny ignored her. "Are you allergic to anything?" she asked Fliss.

Fliss shook her head. Then her mother came into the bedroom and all hell was let loose.

"Was that you screaming in the bathroom, Fliss?" she asked crossly.

Then she saw Fliss's face.

"Oh my poor baby!" she wailed. "What's *happened* to you?"

Fliss had actually started to calm down, but one look at her mum's anxious face made her start crying all over again. It seemed like a good idea for the rest of us to get our stuff together and go to the bathroom.

"I wonder what's going to happen?" said Rosie. "I mean, Mrs Sidebotham's hardly likely to take the rest of us to the audition if Fliss isn't going, is she?"

That was true, but Kenny was more bothered about Fliss's rash.

"Whatever caused it?" she kept saying. "She must have eaten something different, but we only had pizza last night, didn't we?"

Then I remembered.

"The cream!" I yelled. "She slapped that expensive stuff of her mum's all over her face!"

"Good thinking, Lyndz!" Kenny slapped me on the back so hard that I nearly went flying down the stairs.

We all rushed into Fliss's bedroom and told her mum what we thought had happened. Mrs Sidebotham was still fussing over Fliss, but she seemed grateful that we'd got to the bottom of the mystery. At least she knew that it wasn't the plague or anything!

"I'll put on some make-up, darling," she told Fliss, "and no-one will even see those silly blotches."

Fliss smiled a little weakly.

"Right girls, I think you should have breakfast before you get dressed," Mrs Sidebotham told the rest of us. "We don't want any little breakfast accidents on your nice clothes, do we?" She always talks to us like we're about three years old. "Andy's down in the kitchen getting everything ready, so you just run along downstairs while I sort out Felicity's make-up."

We all rolled our eyes. We just *knew* what was going to happen. Fliss would end up looking like a dog's dinner and the rest of us would be so rushed for time we'd look like something the cat had dragged in. Not that I wanted to look good anyway because I wasn't going for the audition, but Frankie and Rosie at least wanted to make an effort. Kenny of course thinks making an effort is wearing a clean pair of trainers!

We all trooped downstairs and were greeted by Andy.

"I hope you're not going to go to the audition like that!" he laughed when he saw us in our pyjamas. "Who's for waffles and syrup?"

"Yes!" we all shouted. At least when we're at

Fliss's we have cool breakfasts! Or at least we usually did... Andy was just about to prepare the waffles when Fliss's mum shouted down:

"I think everybody should have toast this morning. We don't want people feeling queasy at the auditions, do we?"

We all pulled faces.

"Sorry girls," said Andy. "I've got my orders!"

He started popping slices of bread into the toaster.

"Not toast, that's bor-ing!" grumbled Callum, who had just stumbled into the kitchen. "I want waffles. I don't see why I should suffer. I'm not going to a stupid audition."

"Sorry champ, toast's all I'm doing at the moment," explained Andy. "I'll make you some waffles later if you like."

"OK. I'm going back to bed then," mumbled Callum, and shuffled out again. Kenny looked after him enviously.

It didn't take us long to eat our toast. Once we had food inside us we were ready to face the world. But first we had to face Fliss. She sounded very agitated as she called downstairs:

"If you lot don't hurry up and get dressed we're going to be late. Remember what Angel said about getting there early."

"You'd better run along," Andy whispered to us. "You don't want to get Fliss angry – it's not a pretty sight!"

We ran upstairs, where Fliss was waiting for us. She was all made up in pink lipstick and smudgy eyeshadow. You couldn't see the blotches on her skin any more, but you could tell that she was wearing loads of make-up. Her mum was fussing about behind her, putting the finishing touches to a French plait.

"Chop chop, girls!" she tinkled. "I'd like to catch the bus in half an hour, then hopefully we'll be one of the first at the audition."

Fliss went downstairs to have some toast, and the rest of us flew around trying to get ready.

"That's just typical, isn't it?" fumed Kenny under her breath in case Fliss's mum was listening. "Her precious baby has all the time in the world to get ready, and we have to do it all in five minutes!"

"I don't know what you're complaining about," pointed out Frankie. "That's all it takes you anyway!"

It was true that we didn't really need much time. Frankie and Rosie put on a bit of lipstick and some eyeshadow, but apart from that it was just a case of flinging on our clothes and we were ready.

"Very nice, girls!" said Fliss's mum when we got downstairs. "I suppose you didn't need to dress up, did you Lyndsey sweetie? Seeing as you're not actually auditioning."

The cheek of it! I was wearing my best jeans!

The bus stop is virtually outside Fliss's house so we didn't have far to walk.

"Good luck!" called Andy as we left. "May the best girl get the part!"

The bus ride into Leicester is always kind of fun. It's just exciting knowing that you're going into the city. That day though it wasn't quite so great because Fliss's mum kept fussing all the time. Had she got the address of the rehearsal room? Was Fliss quite all right? Were we *all* all right? Did we feel nervous?

"We do now with you twittering on!" muttered Kenny under her breath.

"What was that, sweetie?" said Fliss's mum. "Are you wishing that you hadn't worn your football top?"

Oh-oh. I thought Kenny was going to lose it, but she stayed calm. Even so, I was really relieved when the bus pulled into the Haymarket bus station.

"Right girls, the rehearsal rooms should only be a short walk from here," said Fliss's mum, getting out a map.

We all got off the bus and followed her.

"I hope it's not far!" said Fliss. "I don't want to look all hot and bothered when we get there."

"Don't be silly darling," replied her mum. "It

should be just round this corner. Right, I wonder which one it is?"

Fliss's mum was still looking at her map, but the rest of us knew only too well which building we were looking for. It was the one with millions of girls standing outside.

"Oh my goodness!" squeaked Fliss's mum when she saw the queue. "I didn't realise there would be so many girls."

She wasn't the only one!

"It looks like every ten-year-old girl in Leicestershire is here!" said Frankie. "I didn't realise so many people went to drama class!"

Suddenly there was a whooping and someone called, "Yoo-hoo – over here!"

We scanned the queue, and spotted someone

in lime-green and black near the back who was waving frantically.

"Angel!" we all said together and ran over to her.

"Erm girls, girls – wait for me!" called Fliss's mum, trying to keep up on her high heels.

Angel was as bubbly as ever.

"What an experience this is, girls!" she gushed. "Ah, Lyndsey, you've decided to audition too? Good, I'm very glad."

I didn't have time to explain that I was only there to support the others. The queue had started to move, and we were carried along by it.

"I'm really nervous about this now," whispered Rosie.

"Me too!" mumbled Fliss. Her teeth were chattering even though it was a nice sunny day.

"Now what did I tell you, girls?" boomed Angel. "This is an experience, that's all! Just enjoy it!"

That was certainly easier said than done as far as Fliss and Rosie were concerned. At least Frankie and Kenny seemed happy enough. They were playing football with some of the other girls from our drama class who were further down the queue. Trust Kenny to have brought a ball with her!

You could tell that Fliss's mum didn't approve. She kept looking at them and tutting, and then started telling Angel how Fliss had never liked rough games. Poor Fliss looked dead embarrassed. Especially when Angel said that she liked to see girls enjoying themselves. And to be honest, neither Fliss nor Rosie looked to be enjoying themselves too much. They were either telling each other what a mess they were going to make of their audition, or practising for it under their breath. It was getting on my nerves big time, so I went to join Frankie and Kenny for a kick-about.

We'd been messing about for about half an hour or so, when Angel called out to us:

"Come on girls, we're finally going inside!"

"Yippee!" shouted Kenny sarcastically, and picked up her ball.

The inside of the building was kind of cold. Everyone was queuing down a long corridor, and at the end of the corridor was a set of double doors. It was obvious that the auditions were being held behind them, because there were two women with clipboards who were writing down girls' names and taking them through in groups of five or so.

"I think some of my girls are ready to go in to audition," said Angel. "I'd better go to calm them down. I'll try to see you all before you go in. Best of luck, and remember – enjoy!"

She strode down the corridor, her lime-green and black top fanning out behind her like a peacock's tail.

"Well she's very dramatic, that's for sure!" sniffed Fliss's mum. You could tell that Angel really wasn't her kind of person.

"I can't do this!" whimpered Fliss. "I want to go home!"

"So do I!" stammered Rosie. "I wish we'd never come!"

"Don't be wimps!" said Kenny scornfully. "It's just a laugh, isn't it? Chill out for goodness sake."

"There's no point getting in a flap," reasoned

Frankie. "We're here now, so we've just got to go for it. That's what Angel said – enjoy!"

But Kenny and Frankie's words didn't seem to be having any effect on Fliss and Rosie. They were both as white as sheets. And Fliss's mum looked just as bad – her hands were shaking, and she wasn't even going to the audition.

"Look, why don't we go over it again?" I said to Fliss and Rosie. "I'm sure there must be a room we can go in somewhere."

I looked around. There was a sign for some toilets a little way down the corridor.

"Would it be OK if we went in there to practise?" I asked Fliss's mum.

"I suppose so," she said, and looked more nervous than ever.

"Come on!" I dragged Fliss and Rosie down the corridor.

Behind the door there were two other doors. One led into the toilets and the other led into a small cloakroom.

"In here!" I pushed them into the cloakroom.

89

Fortunately there was no-one else there. "Right, all you've got to say is 'So that's why you spend so long in the bathroom' and hold the bottle like this..." I picked up an empty box from the wastepaper basket.

"But that's not a bottle!" moaned Fliss.

"It doesn't matter," I said, losing patience. "Just pretend you're holding it towards the camera. Then you've got to pull a face and stick your tongue out, remember? Go on, you try it!"

Fliss and Rosie both said their line, but they kind of mumbled it.

"I can't hear you properly," I explained. "You've got to speak clearly, but be natural too. Imagine that you're talking to Callum, Fliss. And Rosie, you can pretend that you're talking to Tiff."

Tiff is Rosie's older sister, and I bet you anything that she spends loads of time in the bathroom looking at her skin.

They both tried again, and it did sound a bit better.

"OK, do it again," I said. "Like this – 'So that's

why you spend so long in the bathroom!'"

I nearly *died* when I realised that someone was earwigging. It was one of the women with the clipboards. I don't know how long she'd been listening to us, but I was sure that she was going to tell us off for being in the cloakroom.

"What's your name?" she asked.

"L-Lyndsey C-Collins," I stammered.

"You haven't auditioned yet, have you?" she asked.

"Nope, I'm not going to, I only…" I started to explain.

I thought she was going to be really angry with me, but all she said was, "Oh, but you might as well now that you're here," and jotted down my name. "I'll make sure that you all go in together, how's that?"

I know it's stupid, but all I could do was nod. Even though I didn't really want to audition at all.

When she'd gone, I said to Fliss and Rosie, "I can always disappear just before you go in."

But I was wrong about that too, because just at

that moment Fliss's mum burst through the doors.

"Quick!" she squeaked, making a grab for Fliss. "We've got to the front of the queue, and if you don't come now we'll lose our place!"

We all ran out towards the double doors. The woman we'd just seen was talking to Kenny and Frankie, who were giving her their names. When they saw us, they gave her Fliss and Rosie's names too.

"And of course there's Lyndsey too!" said the woman.

"Oh, but she's not auditioning," said Frankie quickly, but the woman smiled.

"She is now!" she said and winked at me.

After that, everything was a bit of a blur. I didn't have time to get nervous or anything, because one minute Angel was wishing us all good luck, and the next we were pushed through the doors with a camera in our faces! A really nice man called Greg told us not to be nervous and ran through what we had to say. Then he showed us a mark on the floor where we had to stand. A woman called Stacey was standing in for the older girl who would be in the proper commercial. She said her lines so that we knew where to come in and when to stick out our tongues. And she showed us the bottle we would be holding too. The lighting was really bright when the camera was on, and it took a little while to get used to it. But once we got the hang of it, it was great fun. You felt just like a big famous movie star!

Frankie went first and did a great job – she didn't mess up at all and Greg seemed really pleased with her. Unfortunately you couldn't say the same for Kenny. She giggled so much they had to film her *four* times. That set Rosie off too. I think she was just nervous really. But the second time she said her line it sounded really great, and I could see the woman with the clipboard nodding and writing something down.

Then it was my turn. I went through the line once and I thought that I'd done OK, but Greg said:

"OK, Lyndsey, do you think we could try that again? And can you look at Stacey this time, rather than at the camera? Great!"

So I did it again, and then *again* when he made me hold the bottle differently. I was exhausted by the end!

"You looked like a real professional!" nodded Rosie with approval when I'd finally finished.

"I don't know about that," I replied, mopping my forehead. "I did it wrong enough times!"

Then it was Fliss's turn. She looked absolutely *terrified*. My heart was thumping for her because I knew how badly she wanted to act in this commercial. She looked over to where the rest of us were watching and we all gave her the thumbs-up sign. That made her smile and she started to look a bit more relaxed.

"OK Felicity," said Greg. "You know the words by now. You're standing on your mark so – action!"

"So that's bathroom why you're... sorry!" mumbled Fliss. You could see that she was blushing like a ripe tomato – even through all that make-up.

"Don't worry, let's take it from the top again!" said Greg calmly.

"So that's why, erm, you, erm… sorry, I've forgotten the words!" Fliss was getting really panicky, you could tell.

Greg reminded her of her line and off she went again. This time she said her line perfectly – but dropped the bottle. I felt so bad for her. I mean, there wasn't anything in it of course, but the top did break off, so they had to find another one to use. And all the time Fliss was just standing there, looking as though she wished the ground would open up and swallow her.

To make matters worse, Kenny started to dig me in the ribs.

"She dyed her hair for *this*?" she whispered.

I didn't say anything because I thought that was kind of mean of Kenny. I tried to smile encouragingly at Fliss, but you got the impression that she just wanted to get on with it and get out of there.

On the fourth take Fliss was perfect, which was sort of a relief to all of us.

"I was awful, wasn't I?" she said unhappily when she came over to join us.

"Not really," I tried to reassure her. "We all needed more than one go – apart from Frankie."

"I'm sure they're used to people being nervous," said Rosie gently.

"Or acting the fool!" said Frankie, narrowing her eyes at Kenny.

"Oh no!" whispered Fliss. "The woman with the clipboard's coming over. She's going to tell me how bad I was, isn't she?"

"Don't be daft!" said Kenny, and flicked her hair back in an actressy sort of way. "She's going to tell me that I've got the part!"

We all laughed, but we all sort of held our breath too as the woman walked over to us…

8

"Now I'd just like to say how great you were today," the woman began. "I know everything was a bit strange, but you coped really well. We are calling back a few girls for a second audition and I'm happy to say that..."

We all looked at each other in surprise. One of us must have been chosen! My money was on Frankie – or maybe Rosie.

You could have knocked me down with a feather when she said, "... Lyndsey, we'd like you to come and audition for us again!"

I just couldn't *believe* it. There must have been some kind of mistake.

"Way to go, Lyndz!" shouted Kenny, punching me on the arm.

The woman with the clipboard explained when they'd like to see me again, but I couldn't take it in. Fortunately Angel had reappeared and seemed to know the woman, so she jotted down the details for me. I was in a complete daze.

"So *that's* why they made you do it again!" squealed Rosie. "You hadn't made a mess of it at all!"

"And just think – you weren't even going to audition!" said Frankie in amazement. "It must be fate that you came with us. Isn't that right Fliss? Fliss?"

But Fliss had gone. We all looked round for her, but she was nowhere to be seen. Meanwhile, the room was starting to fill up with the next group of girls.

"She'll probably be out here!" said Angel

decisively. She herded us through another set of doors, and we found ourselves in yet *another* corridor.

There, at the end of it, were Fliss and her mum. Fliss looked as though she'd been crying, and her mum had her arm around her shoulders.

"There you are!" boomed Angel. "The girls thought they'd lost you!"

Fliss looked up but didn't say anything.

"Are you walking back to the bus station?" Angel asked Fliss's mum when we reached them.

Mrs Sidebotham nodded silently.

"I'll walk with you then," she said, leading the way outside. "My car's finally packed up on me, so I'm relying on good old public transport until I pick up my new one on Monday."

Kenny asked her what kind of car she was getting, and they talked about that until we got to the bus station. I didn't join in. I don't really know anything about cars anyway, but I was worried about Fliss. She looked so upset and she hadn't spoken to me at all since the audition. I could tell that she was mad at me for being called back, and I didn't know how to start a conversation without sounding as though I was bragging about it.

"Well, my loves, this is where I leave you!" said Angel as we reached our bus stop. "My stop's over there. I'll see you all at class on Wednesday. Well done, Lyndsey!" And she walked off.

"She's very full of herself, isn't she? Her and her new car!" grumbled Fliss's mum. "She should concentrate on teaching you what you need to know for these auditions, instead of throwing you in at the deep end."

The rest of us looked at each other.

"I don't think it was Angel's fault," said Rosie quietly. "I think we were all a bit nervous, that's all."

"I was only nervous because Lyndz had just gone before me," Fliss piped up. "I wasn't expecting her to be there. It threw me completely, I couldn't concentrate."

"I'm sorry!" I mumbled. I didn't really see how I could be responsible for Fliss forgetting her words, but I wasn't going to argue.

"Well, I'm really pleased for Lyndz," said Frankie, squeezing my arm. "I just hope she does as well in her second audition."

Fliss's lip started to wobble again, so we changed the subject. It was a relief when our bus came. It was kind of busy so we didn't talk to each other much. I was glad really. I wanted to forget the whole audition thing for a while.

When we got back to Cuddington, we had to go and get our stuff from Fliss's and ring our parents so that they could come and collect us.

As we walked up the path, Andy called out, "Well, how did it go?"

But Fliss's mum said, "Don't!" and shut him up with a look.

All the time we were there, Fliss just sulked in her room. She wouldn't speak to any of us – it was dead embarrassing. Kenny tried to jolly her up by tickling her, but Fliss just snapped, "Oh grow up!" and locked herself in the bathroom.

I prayed for Dad to hurry up, but of course we live the furthest away so he was the last to arrive. When each of the others left they gave me an encouraging grin, and said, "Well done!" But I still felt awful.

When Dad finally came, Fliss was still in the bathroom and her mum was trying to coax her out. I heard her telling Fliss it was a stupid commercial anyway, which didn't exactly make me feel great. I was so glad when we were finally driving home.

"You look done in!" Dad commented. "How did the audition go? Did anyone get the part?"

"No, but someone got asked to the second audition," I said.

"That's great! Who?"

"Actually, it was me," I admitted quietly.

Dad nearly swerved off the road he was so surprised. I had to tell him all about it, and then I had to tell Mum and Ben and Spike when I got in. Ben seemed really impressed.

Stuart and Tom just laughed when I told them.

"You? On TV?" they screamed. "It'll be like some horror film!"

Mum made them shut up and they had to do all my share of the chores for the rest of the weekend too. So I guess it wasn't all bad.

It was one thing putting up with my brothers and their stupid comments – I'm used to that. It was different having to get used to Fliss not speaking to me at all. I knew that it was going to be difficult when I went into the playground on Monday morning and Fliss took one look at me and walked off in the other direction.

Kenny said, "Just ignore her Lyndz, she's being a big baby!"

But it wasn't easy. I hate there being any trouble between us, and when the others fall out I always try to sort things out.

"It isn't as though you've done anything wrong," Frankie assured me. "Her ego's taken a bit of a bruising, that's all. She'll get over it."

But to be honest with you, I didn't think she would. And I didn't want her hating me for ever.

Fliss didn't speak to me at all on Monday. And on Tuesday, I could feel her staring at me but whenever I looked at her she just looked away. On Wednesday she was totally awful, and got me into trouble with Mrs Weaver. That made the others mad too. At least she'd been speaking to them, but as soon as they saw how spiteful she was being they decided that they'd do the same to her. It was really, really awful. There was so much bad feeling about – and it was all *my* fault.

I felt really sick when we turned up to drama class in the evening, but Fliss wasn't there which I suppose was no surprise. Angel was really great – she told everyone in the group about the audition, but she didn't make a big deal about it. Then we just went through some improvisation exercises, but my heart wasn't in it. After the class Angel called me to her.

"The audition is on Saturday at the same place and you have to be there at 11 o'clock. Is that all right?" she asked.

I nodded.

"Would you like me to give you a lift?" she asked.

"No, it's OK," piped up Kenny, who had been listening. "We'll all be going together."

"Yeah, for moral support!" chimed in Frankie. "Like Lyndz did for us!"

Frankie, Kenny and Rosie were all standing there grinning like big Cheshire cats.

"That's great!" laughed Angel. "I'll see you all there then."

When we got outside, I took a deep breath and said, "Thanks for wanting to come with me, but I don't think I'm going to go to the audition."

"WHAT?" they all yelled in my face. "You've *got* to!"

"I'm not sure it's worth it," I tried to explain. "Maybe if I don't go, Fliss will speak to me

105

again and everything will be like it used to be."

"Now, I may sound like old whingey-knickers herself," declared Kenny, "but that's not fair. Why should you give up on something just because Fliss doesn't like it?"

"Kenny's right," said Frankie. "If everybody thought like that, nobody'd ever do anything. You've got to go for it, Lyndz."

"Yeah, you're just too nice," agreed Rosie.

I knew they were right, but I just felt so bad about everything. Even Mum knew that something was bugging me when I got home, so I had to tell her what was going on.

"We've never fallen out like this before," I explained miserably. "And it's all my fault. I never wanted to go for the audition in the first place, and it's like I've stolen Fliss's dream or something."

"I think you're just being a bit dramatic," Mum decided, before adding, "which I suppose is quite appropriate under the circumstances!"

Even I had to laugh at that.

"I think your friends are right, Lyndz," said Mum

seriously. "If you would really like to audition again then you've got to do it. If you don't, you'll always wonder what would have happened."

"But what about Fliss?" I asked.

"I think she'll come round soon enough. It's only jealousy, and if I know Fliss she'll have a bee in her bonnet about something else next week. Besides, I think she'd miss your sleepovers too much!"

I knew that Mum was right. I *was* excited about the audition and I *did* want to do it. And I was sure that Fliss would come round in the end – I just wanted her to come round now!

But to be honest with you, that didn't look too likely at all. At school on Thursday and Friday she was as awful as ever. She even started going round with Alana 'Banana' Palmer, who's this dopey friend of the dreaded M&Ms. At least Frankie started talking to Fliss again though. They even teamed up in PE. And I saw Rosie talking to her too. I was glad that the others were friends with her again, but I did feel a bit left out.

After school on Friday I walked to the gates with Frankie, Kenny and Rosie.

"Mum's going to drive me to the audition tomorrow," I told them. "We're leaving at 9.30, so if you want to come with us can you be at my place by then?"

"Sure can!" said Kenny.

"We'll be there!" said Rosie. "See you, Lyndz, must go!"

She and Kenny ran off down the road.

"Will you be OK waiting for your dad by yourself?" asked Frankie. "Only there's something I've got to do."

I said that of course I would, and she ran off as well. Fortunately Dad wasn't too long.

As we were driving home, we passed Rosie, Kenny and Frankie walking down the road – *with Fliss*. I couldn't believe it. I know that it's stupid, but I felt really upset. It was as though they were all going behind my back. I just hoped that they weren't all having a sleepover together without me. The only reason I hadn't organised one was that I knew that Fliss wouldn't come, and I didn't think it would be fair to have one without her.

Seeing all the others together like that really played on my mind all evening. I didn't want to talk about it, so when anyone asked why I was so quiet I just told them that I was nervous about the audition.

"Ooh, get her!" laughed Tom. "She thinks she's a big star already!"

Even when I went to bed I couldn't sleep, and that is unheard of. Mum always jokes that I'd probably sleep through an earthquake! But that night I tossed and turned so much I made myself dizzy. I just couldn't help feeling that I'd split up the Sleepover Club, and that I was the one who'd end up being left out.

9

As I said before, I'm usually really wide-awake and cheerful when it's time to get up. Well the next morning I was mega grumpy. Even worse than Kenny first thing in the morning, and believe me – that's saying something. It was probably because I hadn't slept all night. And also because the first thing I thought about was the others. I knew that I'd upset Fliss and I'd convinced myself that the others had started to take her side in things. So if they'd taken her side, there was no way they were going to show up for my audition.

"Will you stop feeling so sorry for yourself, Lyndsey Collins!" Mum scolded me over breakfast. "If your friends said they'd be here, then I have every faith that they will. Now get a wriggle on for goodness sake, or they'll be waiting for *you*!"

I hadn't even thought about what I was going to wear for the audition. I'd turned up in jeans before and they'd still wanted to see me again, so they obviously weren't too bothered about what I was wearing. Still, I felt that I should make a bit of an effort. The trouble was that I didn't seem to have anything in my wardrobe that was suitable.

"I bet Fliss has loads of clothes that she could choose from," I thought to myself, and then I started to feel miserable all over again.

Eventually I chose a black skirt, a pink T-shirt and my black chunky boots. Getting dressed sort of cheered me up. I'm not really big into make-up so I just wore a bit of coloured lip balm, but even putting that on made me feel more confident. By the time I'd finished getting ready I realised that I was quite excited – and a bit nervous. I definitely had more than a few butterflies in my tummy.

"We'd better think about going soon," Mum called upstairs. "It's almost twenty-five past nine."

I hadn't realised that it was so late. And there was still no sign of the others. I started feeling angry and miserable all over again. We'd never let each other down before.

As I was going downstairs, Tom was just emerging bleary-eyed from his bedroom.

"Off to become a film star, are you?" he yawned. "Well break a leg, or whatever you're supposed to say!"

Dad was having breakfast with Ben and Spike. "I hope it goes well, love," he said.

"Thanks Dad," I said, and gave him a kiss. Ben and Spike were covered in milk and marmalade so I didn't go anywhere near them, I just waved from the door.

Mum was already outside in the van. I could see that she was looking at her watch and peering up the lane, and I knew that she was looking for my friends.

"I told you they wouldn't come," I mumbled.

Mum looked at me kind of sadly and rubbed my arm.

"I see that your friends are as punctual as usual," said Stuart, who was on his way to the farm.

"Shut up!" I shouted. "There's no need to be so nasty."

"What do you mean?" he asked, surprised. "They're here!"

He pointed up the lane – and there were three figures running towards us.

"Sorry we're late!" gasped Kenny. "Dad was called out on an emergency just as we were about to leave."

"And my dad had already gone after dropping

113

me off at Kenny's so Rosie's mum had to bring us here," Frankie explained, all out of breath.

"We didn't think we'd make it!" added Rosie.

"Well we're glad you did," laughed Mum. "We were just about to set off, weren't we Lyndz? Everybody in? OK, here we go!"

I can't tell you how *great* it felt that the others were with me. It didn't feel quite right without Fliss, but I knew that she wouldn't be coming.

There's a gate at the end of the lane that I had to hop out of the van to open. I nearly jumped out of my skin when someone leapt out of a car and ran at me just as I was waiting for Mum to drive through.

"*Fliss*!" I shrieked. "What are you doing here?"

"I thought I'd come with you to the audition," she said quietly. "If that's all right."

"Course it is, silly!" I laughed, and hugged her.

"Mind my new top!" Fliss squeaked, but she was laughing as she said it.

The journey into Leicester went really fast. Apparently the others had persuaded Fliss to come to the audition with them the day before, which is why I'd seen them all together after school. But they'd been expecting her at Kenny's in the morning. When she didn't turn up they thought she must have changed her mind again and didn't wait for her.

"But Mum's car wouldn't start so Andy had to bring me. And when Kenny's mum told me you'd already left we had to come straight here," Fliss explained.

"But what changed your mind in the first place?" I asked her.

"The others made me realise how stupid it was to be jealous," Fliss said, blushing. "I mean, you were the person the advertisers thought was right for their product and I should feel pleased for you. I *do* feel pleased for you."

"And I said I'd dye her hair green if she didn't come!" added Kenny.

"Yeah, right!" laughed Fliss. "Besides, I knew

that you'd need help with your make-up!"

We all screamed with laughter as Fliss took out this amazing palette of eyeshadows and lipsticks.

"What are you *like*?" shrieked Kenny.

I didn't have the heart to tell Fliss that I was happy as I was, so I let her make me up. I actually looked quite good when she'd finished. So by the time Mum had parked near the rehearsal rooms, I felt as ready for the audition as I would ever be.

When we walked into the building this time, there was no-one else around at all. It felt a bit spooky really because everywhere echoed as we walked down the corridors. We followed signs which read: *SPOT AWAY* AUDITIONS THIS WAY. And we ended up in a small room which felt like an old-fashioned classroom.

"Ah Lyndsey, lovely to see you!" It was the woman who had overheard me in the cloakroom last time. "And you've brought along all your friends too – what a nice idea!"

She crossed my name off a list. It seemed

to be a very long list. I started to feel nervous all over again.

"You'll be auditioning at eleven o'clock," the woman told me. "There's nothing to be nervous about. It's just going to be the same as last time except that Alice, the older girl who will be appearing in the commercial, will be filmed with you. That way the director can see how you look together and if there's a chemistry between you."

She showed us all into a room where another couple of girls were waiting with their mothers. They looked dead nervous. They all kept staring at us, and you could tell that they couldn't really work out which of us was going for the audition. That made us all laugh.

"Can you remember your line?" asked Frankie. "Do you want to practise?"

In truth I didn't want to practise. I didn't even want to *be* there. I wanted to be at home – in bed!

"I guess I'd better," I mumbled, so we all huddled in a corner, saying the words together.

"Lucinda Ashby!" called a woman from a

doorway in the corner of the room. In the room beyond, you could see people milling about and the bright lights of the cameras.

One of the girls got up and went out with her mother. The door closed behind them.

"I don't want to do this!" I whispered to the others in sudden panic.

"Well darlings, what does Angel always say?" Kenny suddenly boomed in a loud voice. "Enjoy! It's time you lightened up, Miss Collins. Come on, shoes off everyone, let's go skating!"

The floor was wooden and so well-polished that you could see your face in it. We took off our shoes and went whizzing about all over. It was brill! The girl who was still sitting there looked as though she wanted to join in, but her mum kept scowling at us and glaring at my mum. Mum's pretty cool, not like Fliss's mum thank goodness, so she just ignored us and got on with the knitting she'd brought with her.

You know what Kenny's like – she's a real dare-devil. So she was skidding faster and

118

faster… and before we could stop her, she'd crashed right into a cross-looking girl coming out of the other room and knocked her to the ground. Unfortunately the rest of us couldn't stop ourselves either, and soon there was this enormous pile-up of bodies on the floor.

"Looks like there's been a bit of an accident!" boomed a voice. Angel had appeared from nowhere and was now untangling us all. Mum had rushed over too, and picked up the girl who was crumpled at the bottom of the heap.

"Are you all right, Alice?" Angel asked, flapping her hands around.

"Amazingly, yes I am, no thanks to those stupid girls!" growled the girl, brushing down her clothes. "I was just going to the lavatory. I didn't expect it to be a war zone out here!" She tossed her hair and marched out of the room.

"You just stay here, girls," Angel mouthed to us, and went into the room where the audition was going to take place.

"That was Alice!" squeaked Fliss. "You know,

the other girl in the *Spot Away* advert!"

"Well, that's my chance gone," I decided. "I might as well go home now."

The others obviously agreed with me because they didn't say anything.

Angel came over to join us. "No harm done," she said brightly. "I've just explained about the little accident. It won't count against you, Lyndsey."

I didn't believe that for a minute.

When it was my turn to audition, I'd got myself into such a panic that I started to hiccup.

"Oh no Lyndz, not now!" groaned Frankie. She grabbed hold of my hand and started rubbing it really hard. Fortunately, it seemed to work.

We all trooped into the room with all the cameras.

"I'm not sure that there's enough room for so many people," said one of the assistants. "Some of you will have to wait outside."

"We'll all squash together and be very quiet," Angel assured him.

"Well, OK," he agreed. I think he was a bit frightened of her actually.

I took my place beside Alice, and Greg the director started to set up the lighting.

"You'd better not make a fool of me again!" hissed Alice in my ear. All the time she was smiling so that everyone thought she was being friendly to me. "And don't think you'll get this part either. I'll make sure that you don't!"

Charming!

I remembered Greg from last time – he was really nice. He ran through everything again, and then he shouted "Action!" and started filming. The first couple of takes were perfect. I was really pleased with myself, but old Alice Misery-Chops kept moaning and saying that I was mumbling my lines. So we had to try it again. I was just getting into the swing of it when she stood on my toe.

"So that's why you AARRGGHH!" I screamed.

"I'm so sorry, Lesley!" smiled Alice sweetly, "but you were standing in my space. I didn't expect your foot to be there. I hope I haven't hurt you at all!"

My foot hurt like crazy, but I wasn't going to give her the satisfaction of knowing that.

"Not at all," I smiled at her through gritted teeth. "And my name's Lyndsey."

"OK, let's have a break shall we?" Greg suggested.

I went over to the others.

"She did that on purpose, you could tell!" said Frankie crossly.

"We'll get her Lyndz, don't worry!" Kenny assured me.

Whenever Kenny says anything like that, I *do* worry. And I was very worried *indeed* when Greg said that he wanted to run through the commercial again. Especially as Kenny had wandered off and seemed to be doing something behind Alice's back...

10

I took my place in front of the cameras. A few minutes later I was joined by Alice. She was tossing and stroking her hair, but she completely ignored me. Kenny, Frankie, Fliss and Rosie were standing behind Greg, and I could tell just by the way they were smirking that they had something awful up their sleeves.

"Action!"

I tried to concentrate on my lines, but all the time Alice was twitching about beside me.

"Cut! Are you all right, Alice?" asked Greg. "Do you have a problem?"

"No I'm fine!" she smiled, and started twitching again.

Kenny and Frankie were pulling faces at me, and it took me all my time to keep my face straight. At last Alice looked composed again.

"Action!"

This time, before I'd even begun my line, Alice started scratching her neck.

"Cut!"

I heard Fliss mutter very loudly, "How unprofessional!"

"Alice darling, what *is* going on?" asked Greg. He looked a bit irritated.

Alice had gone quite red in the face and looked as though she was about to cry.

"We'll give it one more try," said Greg, sighing. "And… Action!"

I was just about to start my line when Alice let out an almighty scream.

"A *spider*!" she yelled. "Get it off me!"

A spider was dangling in front of her face. I tried to pull it off her, but she pushed me away.

"Not YOU!" she yelled. "This is all your fault!"

I could see Kenny and Rosie creased up at the back of the room. Frankie was looking a bit alarmed because she hates spiders herself, and Fliss was telling anyone who would listen what a bad actress Alice was anyway. Bad actress or not, everyone was crowded round her – and the cameras were still rolling. It was hysterical. I laughed so much I thought I was going to wet myself. I didn't of course, but my hiccups came back again. I got them so badly that I just couldn't get rid of them. Poor Greg looked horrified. There was no way that we could do any more filming.

"I think we'd better call that a day for you, Lyndsey," said the woman I had seen earlier. She ushered us all out of the room. "You'll be hearing from us in a few days' time. Your mum's given us your address. Thank you for coming."

Angel called "Goodbye" to us, but Mum couldn't get us out of that building fast enough. I thought she was going to be really angry with us, but as soon as we were outside she exploded with laughter.

"That was the funniest thing I've ever seen!" she gasped. "I'd *love* to see that on film. They ought to send it to one of those television outtakes programmes!"

She was laughing so much that tears were streaming down her face, and that set us all off again. It was only when Mum realised that people were staring at us that she managed to calm down.

"Come on, we'd better get out of here!" she spluttered, and we ran giggling back to the van.

When we were on our way home I said to Kenny, "It was you, hic, who put that spider in Alice's, hic, hair wasn't it?"

"Course it was!" she laughed. "I saw it by the door as we went in, and when she was so awful to you, I thought that I'd make use of it if I got the chance."

"Cool!"

We chatted about how awful Alice was all the way back to Cuddington. The others tried various methods of making me lose my hiccups too, but none of them worked.

"Bye, Lyndz! You were a star!" they all yelled as we dropped them off at their homes.

I wondered what Dad would say about the audition when we got back, and Ben. He'd thought it was really cool that I might be on the telly. Now I'd just go back to being his boring sister.

Everyone was in the kitchen when we got in – even Stuart.

"At least I'll get all their stupid comments over with at once!" I thought to myself.

Mum started telling them what had happened, but she couldn't stop laughing so I carried on. But because I was laughing and hiccuping they couldn't understand a word I was saying. By the time we'd finished, everyone was rolling about on the floor.

"Fantastic!" gasped Tom. "I wish I'd been there!"

"Me too!" shouted Stuart, holding his sides.

127

And I knew that Ben thought it was funny because he wouldn't leave me alone all the rest of the day. He kept following me around wanting to play at 'televisions'! Spike just kept saying 'pider' and laughing his head off. The only rotten thing about that afternoon was that Mum made me swallow a teaspoon of vinegar to get rid of my hiccups – and it worked! I don't think I'll be trying that again in a hurry though!

I got the letter about the commercial on the following Wednesday. I knew that I hadn't got the part, but I still had butterflies as I opened the envelope. It was just a standard letter saying that they were very sorry but after much consideration they felt that I wasn't the right person for the part.

"Well, you wouldn't want to work with Miss Sniffy Knickers, would you?" said Kenny when I showed her the letter.

"Nah, that would be awful!" agreed Rosie.

"What did the woman say? They'd have to see if the chemistry was right between you?" asked Frankie. "There was so much *bad* chemistry you'd probably have blown each other up!"

We all roared with laughter at the memory.

"Well, I thought that you were far too good for that advert anyway!" grinned Fliss.

At least we were all still friends. Fliss might not have been so generous if I *had* got the part.

The sad thing about all this is that Angel no longer teaches us drama. She told us at our class that evening that the Production Company had been so impressed with her that they'd offered her a job coaching actors for its commercials. She'll be so good at that, but it means that we're going to miss out on our classes. She promised to try to find us another teacher, but we haven't heard anything yet.

But hey, at least we've got our own play to work on. Which reminds me, we'd better get our skates on. The others will be here in a minute and we want to rehearse one last time before our parents show up. Dad keeps threatening to video the whole thing just in case we have one of our famous mishaps. And the chances are that we will.

Fliss said she'd do all our make-up, so I hope she won't be late. We won't get Kenny to wear any though, not unless it's some of that gory fake blood or something. Frankie said she'd do a plan on the computer saying which scene follows which. We haven't got a script or anything – we just sort of improvise, like Angel taught us – but we do need to know which scene to move on to. You can be a sort of prompter if you like, and look at Frankie's plan. Rosie's organised most of the scenery too, so maybe you should have a word with her to see if she needs a hand. It's a good thing you came, isn't it?!

I can tell by all that shrieking that the others have arrived. And what do you know, Fliss has washed the dye out of her hair and she's back to blonde! Kenny's teasing her about it so I'd better try to calm things down. I don't know about the play, but we seem to create enough drama just hanging out together for a feature length film!

Fliss's TV facial

You will need:

- 1 Avocado
- 2 Slices of cucumber per person

1 Scoop out the avocado.

2 Mash the flesh in a bowl with a fork until you get a smooth paste.

3 Rub the avocado on your face and place one slice of cucumber over each eye.

4 Lie back, switch on the TV and chill out!

5 Wash the avocado off after ten minutes and moisturise.

Now you're all ready for your TV close-up!

FLiSS ✗

Lyndz's TV Star biscuits

You will need:

- 110g (4oz) butter (at room temperature)
- 50g (2oz) caster sugar
- 175g (6oz) plain flour (sifted)
- A baking sheet covered with greaseproof paper
- A rolling pin
- A star-shaped cutter

ASK AN ADULT FOR HELP!

1. Set the oven to gas mark 2/300oF/150oC.

2. Put the butter and sugar in a large bowl and beat together until you have a smooth mixture.

3. Add the sifted flour and mix well.

4. Time to get messy! Using your hands, continue to mix the ingredients together until they form a soft dough.

5. Transfer the dough to a board covered with flour and roll out the mixture until it's about 3-4mm thick.

6. Get your star cutter and cut out the biscuits, then put them on to the baking tray.

7. Bake for 30 minutes.

Lyndz x

Fliss's tips for super-star shiny hair!

- Eat fruit and veggies every day – your body needs vitamins and minerals to grow great hair!

- Exercise regularly – it stimulates circulation and keeps hair follicles in tip-top condition.

- Wear a hat when you're in the sun – your hair can burn too!

- Massage your scalp gently for a few minutes once or twice a week to increase circulation.

- Always wash your hair after you've been swimming to get rid of shine-stealing chemicals.

- Wrap a towel round wet hair and press gently instead of rubbing it dry.

- Dry your hair on the coolest setting to avoid frazzled hair.

FLISS ✗

Have your own super-star sleepover!

- Bring your favourite party clothes, shoes and accessories and dress up like a TV star.

- Bring hair tongs, sparkly slides and hair bands and create your own celebrity look.

- Clear a space down the centre of the room, put on some music and take it in turns to strut you stuff down the catwalk!

- Pick your favourite song, learn the words, and hold your own X-factor or Pop Idol competition.

- Have a terrific TV star sleepover! See you next time – get practising your favourite dance routine…

Lyndz x

Sneak peek!

The SleePover Club

Dance-Off!

It all started a few weeks ago, in the middle of a history lesson (yawn!), when Frankie started squealing. Now Frankie's not one to make a fuss about nothing, so when I heard her making that noise –

"Aieee!"

– and saw her leap out of her chair as if she had a party popper up her bottom, I thought something major had happened, like the M&Ms had put slimy slugs in her socks.

"Francesca Thomas, whatever is the matter?" said our teacher, Mrs Weaver.

Frankie had her fingers in the back of her collar, and she was jumping up and down as if she was trying to shake something out of her clothes.

"What did you put down her neck?" Kenny yelled at the M&Ms, who had been sitting right behind Frankie.

"Laura, sit down!" barked Mrs Weaver.

"Nothing, *stoo*-pid," smirked Emma 'the Queen' Hughes. "We always knew she had ants in her smelly pants."

I could see Kenny seething at that. The M&Ms are so snooty and babyish, it's just gross. Then I saw it. *Plip*! A big splodge of water landing on Frankie's chair. I looked up.

"Mrs Weaver!" I said, pointing up to the ceiling. "Something's dripping!"

It turned out that the classroom roof had sprung a leak right over Frankie's chair, and it had dripped ice-cold water down the back of her neck. Mrs Weaver cheerfully sent Danny McCloud to get a bucket from the cleaners' cupboard. It was weird. She usually got really narked about stuff like this.

Frankie had to move seats. "What's got into Weaver?" she whispered to me as she went by.

"P'rhaps she's won the lottery," I hissed back.

"She wouldn't be giving us a history lesson if she had," muttered Lyndz, who was sitting next to me. "She'd be in Barbados by now."

Just the mention of Barbados made me go all

dreamy – thinking of hot sun, and sandy beaches and palm trees, or whatever they have over there. We used to go on ace holidays abroad when Mum and Dad were still together. Since they split up and Mum started college, though, we can't afford it, worse luck. So here I was, stuck with my dreams on a wet wintry Wednesday in Cuddington.

But not everyone was feeling grumpy. When the bell was about to go for break Mrs Weaver said, with a big smile on her face, "I have some really exciting news."

"I knew it!" I heard Kenny mutter. "She's got engaged to Prince William!"

Lyndz snorted into her pencil case. I thought she was going to get the giggles, but Mrs Weaver gave her a stern look.

Then Mrs Weaver unrolled a glossy poster and pinned it up on the classroom wall.

Fliss gasped. Kenny groaned. The poster said *British National Ballet* on it, and showed a picture of two dancers in sparkly costumes. The woman was standing on her toes and wearing a tiara. No wonder Fliss was excited. Anything princessy is right up her street.

"Are we going on a trip?" asked Alana 'Banana' Palmer, one of the M&Ms' geeky friends.

"Better than that," said Mrs Weaver. "The British National Ballet is coming to us! The company's performing in Leicester at the moment, and two of its dancers will be spending the whole day at Cuddington Primary tomorrow, as part of their 'Theatre in Education' project. They'll take each class for a workshop, and then at the end of the afternoon they'll give a demonstration in the school hall."

"But isn't a workshop where you do woodwork and stuff?" asked Danny McCloud.

"Will we have to wear a tutu and pink shoes?" Alana shouted out.

"Yeah, even the boys!" laughed Frankie.

"Now wait a minute," said Mrs Weaver. "Let me explain. This is a *different* sort of workshop, Danny, and no, Alana, there'll be no special clothes required. You'll just need your P.E. kit. It'll be like those 'Music and Movement' lessons we have instead of P.E. on wet days, except that the dancers will be in charge instead of me."

"Well, this is just *awesome*," said Kenny sarcastically, when the bell had finally gone and the five of us were clustered round her desk. It was a wet break, so everyone had to stay in the classroom. Mr Pownall, the other Year 6 teacher, was supervising us. "Just because Weaver likes ballet, why does she have to inflict it on the rest of us? They'll have us prancing around pretending to be fairies, I bet. I wish we were having a couple of Leicester City players to visit instead." (Oh – Kenny is a major fan of Leicester City Football Club. Did I forget to tell you?)

"It'll be excellent!" said Fliss. "I've never seen real live dancers close-up before. I wonder if they'll bring proper costumes with them..." She took the top off Kenny's new silver pen and started doodling, designing some sort of weird ballet outfit.

"You might get to dance with Ryan Scott, Fliss," suggested Frankie in a silky, tempting voice. "He'd make such a good prince, don't you think?" Fliss looked up with a sudden eager expression, and the rest of us cracked up laughing.

"You're all horrible!" she scowled, turning pink and hunching over her drawing again. She was bent so low, her nose was practically touching it.

"Ohmigosh, forget all that. There's something much more exciting!" said Kenny suddenly, smacking herself on the forehead. "I can't believe I haven't told you yet!"

"What, what?" said Lyndz.

"My folks said we can have a sleepover at my place this Friday!"

"Way to go!" Frankie yelled, and we all did high fives and had a group hug. We hadn't had a sleepover for a few weeks and we'd been missing them badly.

"Let's make it a themed one!" I said.

"Yes – ballet!" said Fliss straight away.

"Noooo!" wailed the rest of us.

"Oh, it's the babies, squealing about nothing again," said a drawling voice right by us. It was the Queen and the Goblin – the M&Ms in other words – leering smugly at us like a couple of Hallowe'en masks.

"Hey, Thomas, I always thought you were a real drip," sneered Emily 'the Goblin' Berryman, nodding at the bucket on Frankie's chair, "but you really proved it today."

A couple of their cronies laughed at this, and it made Frankie fume. "No one could be drippier than you two lamebrains," she said. But the M&Ms had already turned their backs and stalked off across the classroom.

"The M&Ms are asking for it," announced Kenny darkly. "Distract them for me – quick!"

YOU are invited to join Frankie, Lyndz, Fliss, Kenny and me for our next sleepover in...

Dance-Off!

The Sleepover Babes are on a mission to win the school dance competition - no way are we letting our enemies, the M&Ms, dance all over us!

Have **you** got some funky moves? Come along and join the club!

From *Rosie* x